nickelodeon

PAW PATROL™

CHASE IS ON THE CASE!

PaRragon

Bath • New York • Cologne • Melbourne • Delhi
Hong Kong • Shenzhen • Singapore

This edition published by Parragon Books Ltd in 2016

Parragon Books Ltd
Chartist House
15–17 Trim Street
Bath BA1 1HA, UK
www.parragon.com

Based on the teleplay "Pups in a Fog" by Carolyn Hay
Illustrated by Fabrizio Petrossi

ISBN 978-1-4748-5703-1

Printed in China

This book belongs to

_____

_____

One evening, Ryder noticed a problem on the other side of Adventure Bay – the light in the lighthouse wasn't working! Without it, ships could crash into the rocks near Seal Island.

"I'd better tell Cap'n Turbot," Ryder said.

Ryder picked up his PupPad to call the captain.

"Cap'n Turbot, the light has gone out in your lighthouse," Ryder reported. "Can you fix it?"

"No," answered Cap'n Turbot. "I'm out at sea in my boat and the fog is so thick, I can't sail home without the light!"

"Uh-oh," said Ryder.

"Uh-oh is right," agreed Cap'n Turbot. "Plus, there's a big cruise ship full of people due to pass by Seal Island in exactly one hour."

"That ship will need the light, too, or it could crash," said Ryder. "The PAW Patrol needs to get the lighthouse working again!"

Ryder called the pups of the PAW Patrol to the Lookout.
"PAW Patrol, we have an emergency," Ryder told them.
"A thick fog is coming across the bay. Cap'n Turbot is stuck
at sea and the lighthouse light isn't working. We need to fix
it fast, or a cruise ship could hit the rocks near Seal Island!"

"We're ready for action!" Chase reported.
Zuma, Chase, Rubble, Skye, Marshall and Rocky
wagged their tails and waited to be picked for the mission.

"Zuma," Ryder called out, "I need you to take Chase across to Seal Island on your hovercraft."

"Let's dive in!" cheered Zuma, excited to take part in the rescue.

"Chase," Ryder continued, "we can use your searchlight in the lighthouse until Cap'n Turbot gets back."

"Chase is on the case!" the police pup reported.

In two shakes of a pup's tail, Chase and Zuma
were zipping over the waves in Zuma's hovercraft.
Ryder followed close behind on his all-terrain-vehicle.
 Around them, swirls of fog began to appear.
 "The fog is coming in fast," shouted Ryder.
"Let's hurry!"

Suddenly, Wally the walrus popped out of the water in front of them, blocking the way. Ryder glided to a stop.

Wally started jumping in the air and flapping his flippers. Zuma tried to go around him, but Wally would not move.

"Come on, let us pass," Zuma said. "We have to get to the lighthouse to fix the light!"

"This isn't playtime," added Chase.

Then Ryder had an idea. "But maybe it is snack time."
Ryder grabbed a pup treat from his bag and threw
it to Wally, who caught it in his mouth and swam away.
   "Come on, pups," called Ryder, "the fog is almost
at the island!"

When they reached the shore, Ryder, Zuma and Chase could see the cruise ship heading straight for Seal Island. "Chase, we need to get your searchlight to the top of the lighthouse right away," Ryder said.

"I'm on it!" Chase said, looking up the steep hill to the lighthouse. There wasn't a minute to lose.

But when the team arrived at the lighthouse, they found the door was locked!

"We have to find another way in," said Ryder. He looked up and noticed an open window just above them.

"Chase, aim your net just below that window," Ryder said.

Chase opened his Pup Pack to activate his net and then shot it on to the lighthouse.

Ryder climbed up the net and through the window.
"I'm in! Be right down," he called to the pups.
In a flash, he opened the door.
"Great idea, Ryder!" Zuma said.
"Let's roll!" barked Chase as they raced up the staircase.

As Chase, Zuma and Ryder reached the top of the lighthouse, they heard a worried voice over the radio.

"Come in, Seal Island Lighthouse," it said. "This is the cruise ship. We can't see your light. Over."

Chase dashed to the window and shone his searchlight out into the fog.

The light beamed out brightly across the bay.
   "We can see you, Seal Island Lighthouse!" cheered
the captain over the radio. The cruise ship turned away
from the rocks just in time. "Thank you, and out," he said.
   Ryder cheered, and Chase and Zuma barked in celebration.

The light didn't just guide the cruise ship to safety – it helped Cap'n Turbot find his way home, too!

"PAW Patrol – you did it!" he shouted, putting on his sunglasses.

"Um, why are you wearing sunglasses at night?" asked Ryder.

"So I can fix the lighthouse light," said Cap'n Turbot. "Cover your eyes, everyone."

Soon, light shone out over the bay. The lighthouse
was working once more!

"Thanks again, PAW Patrol," said Cap'n Turbot.
"You saved the day, the cruise ship – and me!"

Zuma and Chase barked happily.

"Any time, Cap'n," said Ryder, standing proudly by his pups. "If you're ever in trouble, just yelp for help!"